For tomorrow's voices, Kelly and Danny
—*J.R.*

To my wife, Stella, and my family
—*I.T.*

Clarion Books • a Houghton Mifflin Company imprint • 215 Park Avenue South, New York, NY 10003 • Text copyright © 1995 by Jill Rubalcaba • Illustrations copyright © 1995 by Irving Toddy • The illustrations for this book were executed in acrylic and oil paint on watercolor paper. • The text is set in 16/21-point Meridien. • All rights reserved. • For information about permission to reproduce selections from this book, write to Permissions, Houghton Mifflin Company, 215 Park Avenue South, New York, NY 10003 • Printed in the USA • Library of Congress Cataloging-in-Publication Data • Rubalcaba, Jill.   Uncegila's seventh spot : a Lakota Legend / retold by Jill Rubalcaba ; illustrated by Irving Toddy.   p. cm.   Summary: With the help of the shaman Ugly-Old-Woman, twin brothers defeat an evil serpent, but they find that the powers they gain have a great cost. ISBN 0-395-68970-8   1. Lakota Indians—Legends.   [1. Lakota Indians—Legends. 2. Indians of North America—Legends.]   I. Toddy, Irving, ill.   II. Title.   E99.D1R75   1995   398.2'089975—dc20   93-33350   CIP   AC WOZ 10 9 8 7 6 5 4 3 2 1

Uncegila's Seventh Spot
A LAKOTA LEGEND

Retold by **Jill Rubalcaba**
Illustrated by **Irving Toddy**

CLARION BOOKS / *New York*

Many winters past lived Uncegila,
the evil one,
a serpentlike creature longer than one hundred buffalo.
A row of colored circles snaked down her back.
The seventh circle marked the pathway
to her wicked heart. Victory over Uncegila could be won
only by shooting an arrow
through the seventh spot.
The warrior able to succeed would possess great power.
His tribe would always find buffalo.
His people would never know hunger,
or danger,
or fear.
Even so, few warriors tried.
One look at Uncegila
and a warrior's eyes boiled in their sockets.
Then came madness,
then death.

Uncegila cast her evil spells across the plains,
spoiling the hunting,
poisoning the fields,
and fouling the air.
Until one day the trees,
angered by Uncegila's vile magic,
whispered to twin brothers hunting in the wood.

The brothers hunted grouse.
With his walking stick,
Blind-Twin thrashed the brush,
flushing out the birds.
First-Twin shot them with his bow and arrow.
Blind-Twin waved his stick in front of him.
He neared a group of cottonwood.
The rustling trees spoke.
"Go to the mysterious place," said the brush.
"Find Ugly-Old-Woman, the shaman,
maker of magic arrows that always find their mark."
"Who's there?" Blind-Twin called out.
"The mark is Uncegila's seventh spot,"
the cottonwood whispered in the wind.

That night the brothers plotted.
"Since I cannot see her," Blind-Twin said,
Uncegila has no power over me.
I will shoot the arrows that never miss.
You, brother, must lead me to this medicine woman."

The brothers traveled many moons
with no sign of Ugly-Old-Woman.
First-Twin led.
The dust clogged their ears and noses.
The sun burned the backs of their necks.
But still they searched for the shaman.
And one day they found her.
Ugly-Old-Woman stood outside the entrance of her cave
dressed in beaded buckskin.

The beauty of the beadwork made her
appear even more wrinkled.
But her eyes were in conflict
with her bent unsightly form,
for they suggested great beauty dwelling within.
"Welcome, brothers.
You must be tired and hungry after so long a journey."
There by the fire
were three places, her own
and two waiting for the twin brothers.

When their bellies were full,
and their throats watered,
Blind-Twin told of their quest for Uncegila.
"We need the arrows the cottonwood spoke of.
Will you help us?"
"And what do I get in return
for such a gift?" asked Ugly-Old-Woman.
"We have nothing to give you now
but, should we succeed,
Uncegila's power would be yours."
"I have no need for such powers,
but I am lonely living so far from my people.
I miss the comfort of arms circled around me.
For that I would give you the arrows you seek."
Ugly-Old-Woman gathered the bowls
and took them to the stream to wash.
"She is very ugly," said First-Twin.
"I don't think I could do as she asks."
"No matter," said Blind-Twin.
"I cannot see her ugliness.
It is a small thing to ask,
for the power of Uncegila."

That night Ugly-Old-Woman
smoked the sacred tobacco
from a long narrow pipe
carved from black stone.
Ermine heads and eagle feathers hung from it.
"Great Thunder-Being,
we ask for your protection."
Ugly-Old-Woman closed her eyes
and clutched the amulet around her neck,
an eagle talon.
The brothers sat in respectful silence
while the fire consumed itself
until all that remained
were glowing embers,
red like the eyes
of Uncegila.
Blind-Twin went to Ugly-Old-Woman
and put his arm around her
to warm her,
and it felt good.
He could not see the spell fall away.
He could not see her change.
And First-Twin slept.

"You have freed me from a witch's spell.
My powers will aid you in your quest."
When First-Twin woke
Ugly-Old-Woman turned Beautiful-Young-Girl
emerged from her cave.
First-Twin rubbed his eyes.
The air around her sparkled and danced—
so rare was her beauty.

For four days
the twins purified themselves
in the blanketing heat of the sweat lodge.
On the fourth day
Ugly-Old-Woman turned Beautiful-Young-Girl said,
"You must leave tomorrow.
Tonight we feast."
That night
the spirits of many medicine men,
generations of great shaman,
joined them at the circle fire.
Ugly-Old-Woman turned Beautiful-Young-Girl
lifted a quiver of arrows
from the altar of buffalo hides
and painted skulls.

As she handed the seven arrows to Blind-Twin
she warned him,
"These magic arrows
must never touch the ground.
Before you sleep
place the quiver on a tripod
facing the rising sun.
The sun's first rays will feed them."
To First-Twin she gave a shield
made from hardened buffalo skin.
On it was painted a turtle.
"The turtle is hard to kill.
Like the turtle,
you must draw beneath this shield.
it will protect you
from Uncegila's deadly stare."
From her belt
she withdrew two amulets
made from rattlesnake skins.
"Both of you are now cousin
to the rattlesnake.
Strike swiftly,
and silently."

Then Ugly-Old-Woman turned Beautiful-Young-Girl
spoke to the braves one last time.
"Uncegila will try to trick you.

When she is dead cut out her heart.
The heart will speak.
It will ask you to do many things.
The first request will be an evil trick
to restore her life.
You must not obey it.
But from then on you must always do exactly as the heart asks.
Then the power will be yours.
Above all, no one else must ever look upon the heart
or the power will come to an end.
The Wise-One-Above smiles on your mission."

The next morning Ugly-Old-Woman turned
Beautiful-Young-Girl
was gone.
The brothers started out
for the lifeless lake
where Uncegila slept.
Each day brought them closer.
Blackened trees groped the sky
with crooked fingers.
Steam rose from the edges of the lake
where Uncegila lay.

The brothers waited
behind an outcropping of rock.
"When Uncegila's horn breaks
the water's surface
I will tell you, Blind-Twin.
You must slowly count to four
before letting all seven arrows fly."
They did not have long to wait.

A gurgling and sucking sound,
like a foot being pulled from the mud,
disturbed the silence.
Uncegila's horn broke the water
sending circles across the inky lake.
The foul water heaved and rolled.
First-Twin covered himself with the turtle shield.

"Now, brother."
Blind-Twin counted.
"One."
Uncegila's eye fastened on Blind-Twin.
When her evil stare failed,
she shrieked with rage.
Blind-Twin grasped the first arrow
with trembling hands.
"Two."
Uncegila exhaled a plume of flame so hot
Blind-twin's eyebrows curled and fell as ash.
He raised his bow toward the waves of heat.
"Three."
Uncegila's fury grew.
Beating her great wings
she rose above the lake,
swirling the fetid air
around Blind-Twin.
Blind-Twin drew taut his bow.
"Four."
He shot his arrows one after another
until his quiver was empty.
Ugly-Old-Woman turned Beautiful-Young-Girl's arrows
flew straight and true.
Every arrow hit the seventh spot.

Uncegila's shrill death screams
shook the earth and shattered boulders.
Her thrashing tail brought the black lake
raining down on them.
When the last echo faded away
the brothers scrambled down
to where Uncegila lay
and cut her open,
exposing her heart.
An icy blast spewed from her side.
Billows of steam puffed around
the pulsing red crystal.
The brothers worked quickly now,
removing the throbbing heart
and wrapping it in buffalo skins.
A muffled voice
from inside the skins
called to the twins,
"Put the tips of the horns from my head in my wound."
First-Twin hacked off the horns
and buried them under rocks,
far from the body of Uncegila.

The heart spoke again.
"Blind-Twin,
take my blood
and bathe your empty eye sockets."
Blind-Twin cupped his hands
and brought them to his face.
Eyes grew in the sockets
where none had been before.
Blind-Twin became One-Who-Sees.
The brothers hastened to return to their village.

A sacred lodge was built to house Uncegila's heart.
Only the twin brothers entered the lodge.
The powers of the heart
led the tribe to buffalo
and fresh water
and fertile land.
The village prospered.
They never knew hunger
or danger
or fear.

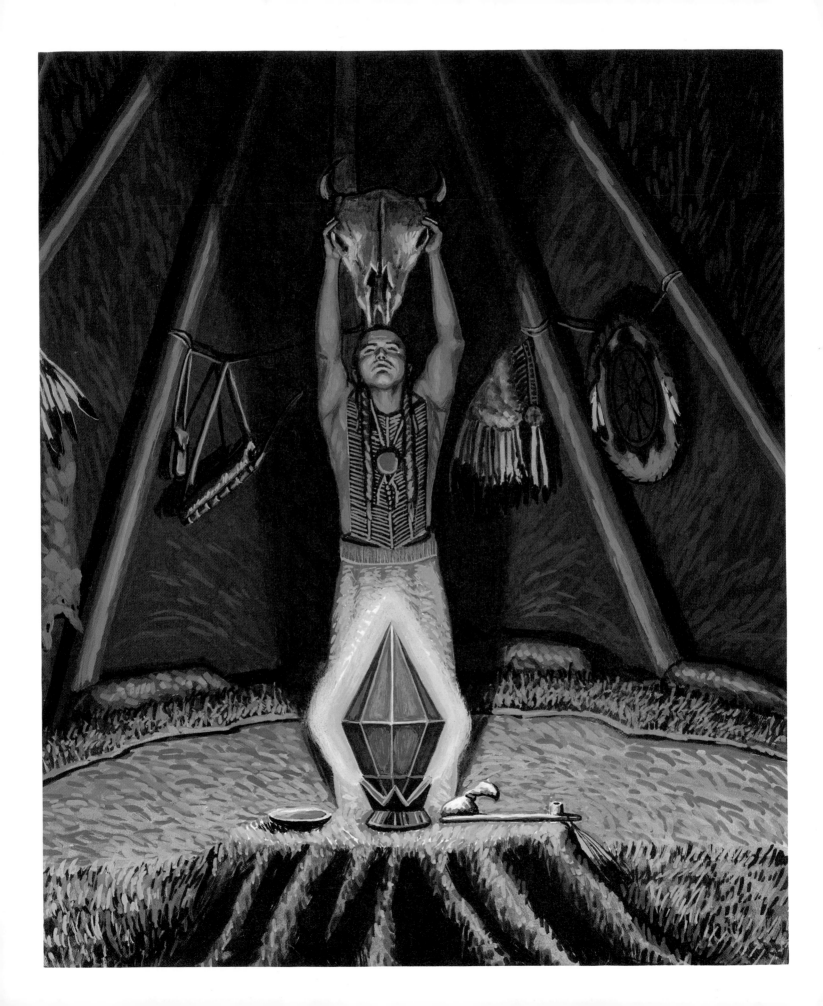

First-Twin took many wives
and lived comfortably.
One-Who-Sees searched for
Ugly-Old-Woman turned Beautiful-Young-Girl,
but not even the great powers
of the pulsing crystal heart
could find her.

The heart demanded many ceremonies.
Summer days once spent tracking game
were now consumed feeding the voracious heart.
Winter nights once spent listening
to tales told by the old ones
were now wasted heeding the heart's commands.
"The challenge of the hunt is gone,"
First-Twin complained.
"I have heard our people whisper.
They grow tired of the heart's endless whims,"
One-Who-Sees replied.
"Perhaps the villagers would like to see the heart."
As he spoke First-Twin smiled, remembering
Ugly-Old-Woman turned Beautiful-Young-Girl's warning.
"Many are curious."
"It is time to call a council," One-Who-Sees said.

The villagers lined up
outside the sacred lodge.
As each member of the tribe
entered the lodge
the heart shone brighter
and brighter.
When the last person
added his gaze
to all the others
the heart exploded.
The fate of the village was no longer certain.
They would feel hunger,
and face danger,
and know fear.
Uncegila would no longer spoil the hunt.
Her heart would no longer feed them.
Now they could grow strong
and resourceful.

One-Who-Sees lifted the lodge skin
and faced the plains.
He shielded his eyes from the sun's glare,
and watched a woman approach along the deer trail
using her root digger for a walking stick.
Though he had never seen her before
there was something familiar.
Even from where he stood
he could see that she was very beautiful.
The air around her sparkled and danced.
His fingers that once served him as eyes
itched with the memory of the pattern
of the beaded buckskin
and the eagle talon that hung from her neck.
One-Who-Sees hurried to ready a second place by his fire.

Author's Note

When the tide of darkness comes in on late afternoon and the winter's winds howl, I hear spirit voices. A chorus of voices centuries old telling their stories. Telling their children and their grandchildren and their great-grandchildren the stories that record the history of their tribe and their ancestors. Stories that teach religion and moral conduct. Stories that explain thunder and rain, day and night, life and death. And then there is silence.

The nineteenth-century Indian Wars brought death to the elders, the keepers of the stories, in numbers so staggering the young were bereft of teachers. Voices silenced. Histories lost. In a desperate effort to save the past, missionaries transcribed the words of those few remaining village elders. Children were coaxed to tell the stories told to them by their fathers and grandfathers. Judges even sentenced criminals to collect the legends of their people as retribution for their crimes. What they were able to save is but a fraction of what was lost. Voices haunt us with the stories no longer told on a winter's eve.

Uncegila's Seventh Spot is a Lakota legend. Handed down generation to generation, polished with each roll of the tongue, like a pebble caught in the ocean wave. The legend shares the ancient wisdom that wealth is sweet only through effort, and slavery is too high a price to pay for security. The legend came to me through the efforts of Richard Erdoes who recorded the words of the medicine man George Eagle Elk in *American Indian Myths and Legends.* The story has been passed on, a voice heard. Tell the stories, tell them to your children and your grandchildren and your great-grandchildren. Add your voice to the chorus. Polish the stone.